Hockey Practice

written by
Diana Geddes

illustrated by
Kate Salley Palmer

KAEDEN BOOKS™

We practice hockey at the rink. First, we skate around the rink to warm up. Next, we skate in circles. Then we take turns passing and shooting the puck. We are ready to play.

3

The puck is dropped on the ice and practice begins. We move the puck along the ice with our hockey sticks. We keep our heads up. Pass the puck!

5

We bump into each other, and we fall on the ice. The puck is spinning. Pass the puck!

The puck flips off the hockey stick.
It slams into the boards. We get the rebound.
Pass the puck!

We break away from the others. We skate right down the middle toward the goal. Shoot the puck!

It goes past the goalie and slams into the net. We score a goal!